THIS BOOK BELONGS TO

_____

Edited by Susan Cunningham at Perfect Prose Services

Illustrated by Andrew Painter

Book design by Callum Knight

On the Bus

An Autism Story

Illustrated by Andrew Painter

By Callum Knight

& L.B. Arthur

It was a grey and rainy day in Kingswood, where Daniel lived with Thor, a golden retriever who was his best friend, his sister Emily, and his mum and dad.

Daniel was busy playing with his toy cars when his mum called, **"Come on, Daniel. It's almost time to leave. Please put away your toys, and I will fetch your jacket."**

"Not yet. I'm not ready." said Daniel.

Daniel always lined up his toy cars on a road that he'd made himself using leftover cardboard from an old cereal box and **big**, **bright** felt-tip pens.

His mum looked through the window at the heavy rain splashing outside.

"It's too far to walk in this weather, so let's take the bus," she said. "You have five more minutes. I'll put the timer on."

She packed a bottle of water, some snacks, Daniel's headphones to help him when there was too much noise, and his favourite book.

Then she handed him his bright yellow jacket.

But Daniel refused to put it on, not because he was being naughty, but because he already felt too warm and he knew that the jacket would make him even hotter.

When that happened, it felt like electric shocks exploding all over his body, like fire. But Daniel couldn't find the words to explain, so all he could do was shout and shake his head.

"N O O O O O."

"All right, why don't you wear it like a cape instead?" said his mum.

Daniel agreed and pretended he was a **SUPERHERO.**

But it wasn't long before he had cooled down so much that suddenly he was FREEZING.

By the time they reached the bus stop, Daniel's jacket was so heavy on his shoulders that it felt like it had come alive and was trying to squash him to the ground.

That made him so **angry**, that he flung his jacket down.

A tall man waiting at the bus stop shook his head. **"What a naughty boy,"** he said, looking at Daniel.

But Daniel's mum understood that sometimes clothes made him feel uncomfortable.

So, she picked up his jacket and explained to the man that Daniel was autistic and sometimes he did things that other people might not understand.

When the bus arrived, Daniel waited patiently for everyone to get off before he climbed on.

He wanted to sit by the window and count all the cars that drove by, but the bus was too busy, and the window seats were already taken.

Daniel's mum sat down and held him on her lap.

Next to them was an old lady. She was friendly and smiled at Daniel.

But he didn't smile back. All he wanted to do was run away because the lady's perfume was so strong that he could almost taste it.

Suddenly, he felt panicked and couldn't breathe properly, so he became restless and shook his hands.

"Do you want your headphones, Daniel?" asked his mum.

But Daniel didn't want his headphones; he wanted to breathe fresh air.

He quickly scrambled off his mum's lap and ran to the front of the bus because he needed to get away from the strong perfume smell.

He jumped up and down and waved his arms around as he looked for an open window.

Daniel's mum rushed to bring him back and sat him on her lap again.

But he wasn't happy, so he hid his face inside his jumper.

The old lady looked shocked. **"What is the matter with him?"** she asked.

Once again, Daniel's mum explained.

"My son is autistic, and sometimes he does things that I don't always understand."

She hugged Daniel tight and said, **"Do you want to press the big red button to tell the driver we are getting off at the next stop?"**

Daniel gave his mother a wide smile. **"Yes, please,"** he said.

That was his favourite part of the journey!

What colour is your jacket?

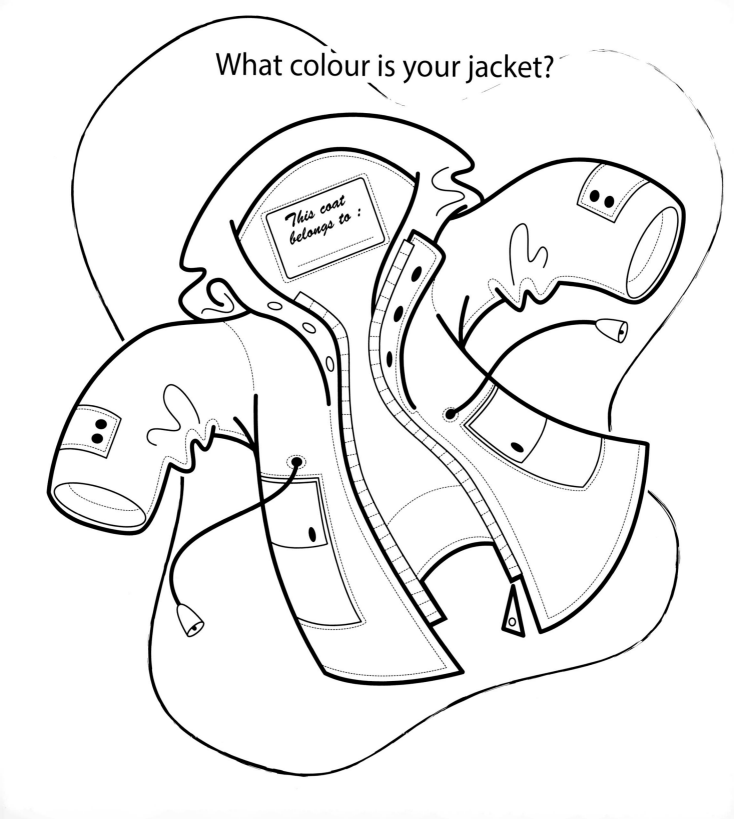

Can you spot the 15 differences?

You can find the answers on the back. No peeking!

Answers to Spot the Difference

Ball in Daniel's hand

Daniel's eyes

Daniel's star logo

Daniel's shoe sole

Daniel's shoelace

Thor's dog lead in Daniel's hand

Thor's nose has changed colour

Thor's ears have changed colour

Thor's tail is gone

Flowers in the foreground

One big cloud

Missing one flying bird

One butterfly changed colour

Tree on the left

Thor's hammer tag is missing